SUNBEAM
in Paradise

CHAS WILLIAMSON

A Women's Christian Fiction Second-Chance Novella

Print ISBN: 978-1-64649-380-7

eBook ISBN: 978-1-64649-369-2

Year of the Book
135 Glen Avenue
Glen Rock, PA 17327

Companion Novella to
Starlight in Paradise

Chapter One

I t was Monday night, and like usual, Lexi was hosting the recreation league volleyball game. She'd had the idea several months ago as a way to battle solitude. But this evening was different. Lexi's boyfriend, Christian, was in attendance. Since he opened his restaurant, Christian had skipped the weekly games. She had coaxed him back for several reasons. First, Christian needed a break from his sixteen-hour days running his business. While that was true, it certainly wasn't the main reason. Lexi had a question in her heart that begged to be answered.

One of her teammates set the ball high above Lexi. She spiked the sphere and her kill sealed the victory. Lexi smiled. "That's game. We still have time to play another match. Let's switch sides and volley for serve."

She touched Christian's hand as they relocated to opposite sides of the net. And once again, he lined up next to Tracilyn. You know—the woman who once held Christian's heart. All night, Lexi had observed how Christian couldn't keep his eyes off of the older woman. Determining if there was still something between Christian and Tracilyn was the main reason why Lexi had invited Christian to attend. That pair had a history, and although both boldly voiced to her that their relationship was over, Lexi could sense a deep, mutual attraction still existed.

"I don't understand this. I try to be so kind," Lexi muttered to herself. She knew she was much more attractive than Tracilyn, but looks weren't everything. Lexi worked hard to be kind and sweet, but that didn't seem to matter. The realization that the bond between Tracilyn and Christian was still strong hit her like a sucker punch.

Because the two were spending so much time watching each other instead of concentrating on the game, Lexi decided to drop a soft lob between the pair. The move caught them both off guard.

Tracilyn shifted to dig the drive, but instead somehow managed to step on the ball. Her leg rolled out from underneath her and the older woman fell to the floor with her full weight on her limb.

The snap of Tracilyn's broken bone was nauseating. Even more sickening was how quickly Christian was by the lady's side. Seemingly without even a second glance at Lexi, he carried Tracilyn to her van and drove the injured woman to the hospital.

Lexi watched the tail lights disappear into the distance. As they dwindled into the night, one thought invaded Lexi's mind. Just like the lights on the van, her love story with Christian was also fading.

As she stood gazing into the darkness, the other players departed. Lexi turned so she could put the equipment away. *Great. I'm stuck cleaning up by myself.*

"Ma'am, would you like a hand putting the nets away?"

Lexi turned to take in the man who had just spoken. He'd been attending the weekly games for about a month. His Southern accent hinted at charm. He was wearing a blue tee shirt that had *Wentworth Tool and Die* emblazoned across the front. She answered, "That would be nice."

He offered his hand. "My name's Clifton McCallister, but you can call me Cliff."

"Nice to meet you. I'm Lexi."

His handshake was firm and his skin warm. "I 'member. We met a couple of weeks ago."

Together, they walked inside. With Clifton's assistance, it didn't take long to stow everything. She would be able to leave as soon as the floors were swept and the trash collected.

Lexi's mind focused on the one task remaining. She needed to go see Tracilyn's daughter, and explain to her what had happened. Lexi only hoped that the younger woman wouldn't see or question the pain Lexi knew would be evident on her own face.

Tonight's events were foremost on her mind as she emptied the waste containers from the restroom. "It's almost funny. I waited and waited, giving them every chance to make it work."

Lexi had met both Christian and Tracilyn on Easter at the Campbell family's celebration. While

Lexi had been attracted to the man immediately, she sensed something was in the air between Christian and Tracilyn. While sitting on the sidelines, Lexi watched the pair's relationship blossom, fully bloom and then wither on the vine. After the eulogy to their partnership was all that remained, then and only then, did Lexi allow herself to fall for Christian.

"Maybe I didn't wait long enough."

"Not sure what you mean, ma'am."

Spinning toward the owner of the voice, Lexi found herself facing the man named Clifton. "I'm sorry. I was so lost in thought, I forgot you were here."

Clifton's expression changed and his Caribbean-blue eyes seemed to soften. "I know it ain't my business and I apologize for stickin' my nose where it don't belong, but I hope y'all know it's not your fault."

What? How could he know what she was feeling? "I beg your pardon?"

His left hand started to move toward her right shoulder, but stopped before contact. Lexi watched it return to his side.

"That woman who got hurt, that's not on you. She was the one who messed up. The lady should have been payin' more attention to the game than the guy who was next to her."

Aha! I wasn't the only one who saw it. "Maybe. But still, I feel bad."

"Perhaps you shouldn't. One of the things my mama taught me is that we're only responsible for ourselves. You can't control what others think or do, even when it makes you feel pain." His face changed and an aura of sadness settled like a cloud over the room.

"Thanks, but I still regret it happened." Lexi closed the trash bag in her hand. "I need to get going, so I'm going to lock up now."

"I'll walk out with you." He gently removed the plastic sack from her hand as they headed to the door. After depositing the trash in the hopper, he returned to her side and ambled along in the direction of her Kia.

"You don't have to do this, Cliff. My car's right over there."

"Maybe, but what kind of gentleman would I be if I didn't accompany you on a dark night?"

His presence was comforting, though unnecessary. When she squeezed the fob to unlock the vehicle, he swung the door open for her. Slipping into the front seat of her ride, he closed it and backed away a step or two.

"Ma'am?"

"Call me Lexi."

"Okay. Lexi, I can see tonight's incident bothers you. If you want to talk about it, please feel free to call me. You have my number. It was on the registration form. And thank you for what you do."

"What I do? I don't understand."

"This whole volleyball thing. It's much more than a way to get exercise. It surely takes the lonely outta the week. I hope y'all have a great rest of the night."

Clifton turned and walked across the parking lot to a huge Ford truck. It reminded her of the souped-up pickups she'd seen in some of the country music videos. A rollbar with a bunch of fog lights sat behind the cab. A South Carolina license plate was centered on the back bumper, between Luke Bryan and Jason Aldean bumper stickers.

A text alert sounded on her cell. Glancing down, she read it.

> At the hospital. X-rays confirmed both bones in her left leg broken. Waiting for some specialist to come in and cast it. Will text again when we leave. Chris

Shaking her head, Lexi shifted the car into drive. Clifton's vehicle was gone. For a second, she reflected on the man with the accent of the deep South. It seemed his presence had been the sole comfort this evening, but now the grim task remained. She needed to go see Tracilyn's daughter, explain what had happened, and give her a hand getting ready for when the injured woman returned from the hospital.

Once again, the memory of what she noted between Christian and Tracilyn reared its ugly head. There was but one thing to do.

"Lord, I need your help. I'm struggling and feel like I'm in a no-win situation. Please send me help… or a miracle. Thank you."

For whatever reason, that simple prayer lifted her heart. And words filtered into her mind, possibly from God? *Okay, my child. How about I send you both?*

Chapter Two

I t had been several weeks since the event where the older lady hurt herself during the game. Clifton watched the pretty blonde closely. At first the girl named Lexi seemed depressed, and it seemed to grow deeper each time they met. Sensing she needed space, he didn't push her. Honoring her apparent desire for solitude, Clifton hung around long enough to help clean up after the matches and then made sure she made it safely to her car.

Tonight, Miss Lexi looked spent. There were bags under her eyes and she shuffled as she walked. Maybe it was his imagination, but he believed he could read the signs. Her appearance reminded Clifton of how his own had been, just before he'd moved north. The sad aura ended when Clifton finally admitted defeat. When he grew tired of seeing his brother and ex-girlfriend galivanting around town, smearing his name as well as his reputation. Now, South Carolina was just a distant image in the rear view of his life.

The pretty lady seemed subdued during the games. Gone were her funny little jokes and sweet laughter. After everyone left, they cleaned up together without a word spoken between them. He could sense she was not only tired, but was struggling with something.

Clifton had overheard a few of the other players gossiping about Miss Lexi, and how her boyfriend ran off with the other woman. If the rumor mongers were correct, he'd seen the incident in the first person. It happened when the old gal broke her leg that evening.

The chill in the air made him shiver. Miss Lexi's head was down as they walked to her Kia. Just before they arrived, she stopped dead in her tracks.

"Somethin' wrong, ma'am?"

"Did you see me lock the doors to the barn?"

"No, I didn't."

"Was I carrying my purse when I got here?" He had been the first to arrive and had warmly greeted the girl.

"You were, but I remember you returned to your car for somethin'. I don't believe you had it after that."

Her eyes searched his and she wrinkled her nose. She was so adorable that he almost chuckled.

Miss Lexi peered in the rear window. "Crap. I remember now. I came out to get my water bottle and there's my purse—just sitting on the seat. Inside it are my keys." The girl slammed her fist against the roof and a sob escaped.

"Tell me how to help you."

"I can't lock up the building. And of course, I'm not even able to open my car door or even call for help because my phone's in there. I need to find a rock so I can bust the window."

He couldn't help it. Clifton chuckled.

She spun to face him. "And you stand there laughing at me? What is wrong with you?"

"Ma'am, I'm laughing at the situation, not you. Let's figure it out together. Do you have another set of car keys?"

"Yes. They're safely stored in my apartment."

"Good. Since I assume your room keys are most likely in your bag in the back seat, do you have another way to get into your apartment?"

She gazed at him, apparently in wonder. "The neighbor lady and I exchanged keys in case of an emergency."

"Then why don't I drive you there so you can pick up your keys, then I can bring you back. Would that help?"

"It would, but first... can you tell me why you'd do this for me?"

He felt the smile on his face grow wide. "I come from the South, ma'am. This is how my mama raised me. You see, down home, we take pride in helpin' each other. It's what the good Lord would want us to do."

"I grew up in the Rockies. My parents taught me to be careful."

Perhaps she doesn't trust me... yet. He extracted his cell, unlocked the screen and handed the device to her. "Here."

"What's this about?"

"Call somebody, anyone you want. I could tell all evening somethin's been wrong. The last thing you need is more stress. It won't offend me if you call a cab or a friend. But if you're thinking you might have enough faith in me to give you a lift, why don't you at least let a friend know I'm taking you. Give them my license plate number or whatever else might make y'all feel less frazzled. I don't want you to worry none."

"Cliff, it's not that…" She extended her hand and offered the phone back to him.

"Nope." He shook his head. "At least call your neighbor lady so she'll know you're coming."

For the first time all evening, Miss Lexi smiled. "This is the nicest thing that's happened to me all day. Like God sent you here to help me."

Clifton snickered. "That's another little thing my mama always said. Ain't nothing that happens down here that the good Lord don't plan." He walked over and opened the passenger door to his pickup. "My lady, your Lariat awaits."

A little laugh escaped her lips. "Don't you mean chariot?"

"I see you got a lot of learnin' to do when it comes to me. I'm talking about my Ford truck."

"And there's a few things I need to teach you as well." He'd never seen Miss Lexi smile this way.

"Such as?"

"Specifically, how to determine when I'm teasing you in return. My first vehicle was a four-wheel drive truck. Of course, I didn't need a step-ladder to climb in the cab. Why in the world do you need such large tires?"

"Well, you get to see everything from up here." He shot her a wink. "After driving that little thing you got parked there, it's time you moved up in the world." He offered his hand to steady her when she stepped on the running board to climb in.

Turning in the seat so they could see each other's faces, the lady's expression sobered as she studied him. "Maybe it is."

Chapter Three

L exi studied her reflection in the mirror. For the first time in quite a while, the image hinted at an emotion she'd assumed was gone from her life forever—happiness. The modest, yellow dress clung to her trim frame in a way that accentuated her figure, yet made her feel elegant. She'd even taken the time to braid her hair, all for Clifton.

Lexi's mind drifted back to the prior evening. The man was correct. From the bucket seat in his jacked-up truck, she had a clear view of the world—and perhaps a hint there might be a bright spot waiting for her beyond the horizon.

Their conversation had been soft, but non-stop. He wanted to hear all about her world and she obliged. She'd held back the part involving Christian. It seemed Clifton had also kept his cards close to his chest involving his romantic past, despite his self-depreciating humor.

After retrieving both her keys and then her car, Clifton had followed her home and walked her to her door. Her mind drifted back to their conversation.

"Thank you for all your help tonight."

"Ma'am, the pleasure has been all mine."

"Cliff, why do you call me ma'am? It's okay to call me Lexi."

"I mean no harm. It's like a badge of honor. I never met a lady like you."

Lexi hadn't wanted the evening to end. *"Would you like to come in for a while?"*

She'd been surprised by his hesitation. *"I certainly would, but the hour's getting late and besides, it might not be proper."*

"What do you mean?"

"Me coming in."

"Why?"

"You see, Lexi, I got my heart broke real bad. Maddie tore up my world and I swore I'd never let a woman git close to me again. But there's somethin' very extraordinary about you. Now maybe nothin' will ever come of it, but I'm not gonna take that chance. I plan on treating you with every ounce of respect I can find. That's the reason why I can't come in tonight."

"Would you like to talk about what happened with her?"

"At some point, but tonight, it's like that girl, or any other, never existed. At least when I'm close to you."

"Then what's next?"

"If you have it in your heart, how 'bout dinner tomorrow night?"

It took everything Lexi had not to kiss his cheek before he left. Instead, she watched in disbelief as his lips grazed her fingertips. She hadn't wanted him to leave and immediately missed him when he'd gone. But that was last evening. Clifton would be here any moment.

When the doorbell rang, she chanced one more glance in the mirror before slipping her coat on her shoulders. And that's when Lexi noted it. The woman reflected in the glass revealed something she hadn't seen on her face in a long while—total bliss.

***

Clifton offered his hand and then turned his head to the side when Miss Lexi swung her legs out before climbing from the cab. It wasn't that her dress was too short, but he wanted to offer her as much courtesy as he could. *This lady is special.*

He couldn't help but notice that she didn't remove her hand from his as they walked into the restaurant. Okay, a chain steakhouse wasn't the ideal choice for a first date, but when he'd asked what her favorite food was last evening, Miss Lexi mentioned how much she loved filet mignon.

"This is very nice of you. We can split the check if you'd like." Her blue eyes sparkled tonight.

"Naw. This is my treat."

"Thank you. I know you mentioned what you do, but could you tell me again?"

"I'm a journeyman tool and die maker. That means I build tools, maintain dies and other implements that form flat metal into useful objects. I served a five-year apprenticeship to learn my trade."

"Oh, that explains the *Wentworth Tool and Die* shirt you wear Monday evenings. Is that where you work?"

Clifton laughed softly. "Nope. Mama gave me that shirt for Christmas two years ago as a gag gift. Did you ever hear of an old television show called *Dallas*?"

"My mom used to watch their re-runs when I was younger. Were you a fan?"

"No, but Mama was and still is. Actually, you could call her a super-fan. I got named after one of the characters. There was a bad boy named Cliff Barnes. One of the companies he owned made things for the oil rigs. According to the storyline, the company was named Wentworth Tool and Die."

Her nose wrinkled when she laughed. "What? Wait! Your mother named you after a villain?"

"She kind of had a crush on the actor who played that part. His real name was Ken Kercheval."

"That might explain it. Do you have siblings?"

His face warmed. "Yes. Two sisters, Sue Ellen and Pamela—real nice ladies. And a brother named John Ross—J.R. for short. We's all named for characters on the show."

Miss Lexi studied him. "I'm getting a bad vibe between you and your brother. Am I wrong?"

He paused, taking a moment to search Lexi's face. "No, ma'am. J.R. is the family scoundrel, always causing problems, especially for me. Just like the characters were in the series, in real life the two of us are arch enemies."

"Why?"

"We're like Cain and Abel—as different as brothers can be. I prefer huntin' and fishin', while he enjoys golf. When it comes to me, he acts like everything's a game and he has to win. I think he'd gladly cut off a hand to git the better of me."

"Wow. What's he do?"

"J.R.'s a lawyer, not one of the respectable ones, but of the ambulance chasing variety. He always has to have his own way and doesn't care who he runs over to get it."

"I'm sorry."

Clifton studied his sweet tea and then lowered his voice. "Boy, does he love when it's me he's getting the upper hand on. J.R.'s been jealous since the day I was born because he was no longer the only apple in Mama's eye."

He waited until Miss Lexi was looking directly into his eyes before adding, "He's the main reason I left South Carolina and moved to Pennsylvania."

Chapter Four

T he server arrived with a food tray and a stand. After the man delivered their plates, he asked them to make sure their steaks were prepared as they wished. They both replied affirmatively, so the man departed.

An awkward silence seemed to engulf the table. *I've said too much.* Clifton hadn't even had the opportunity to explain in greater detail. He was about to slice his steak when the touch of Miss Lexi's hand on his arm startled him. "What did he do to you, to make you leave?"

Her steak sat there untouched. The lady's full attention was focused on him.

After she offered an encouraging smile, he said, "Maddie Brown and me were a couple since sixth grade. Inseparable, best friends, partners in crime—however you want to describe it. She was never much to look at when she was younger, but I loved her. Skinny as a rail, buck teeth sticking out with a wide gap between them—few men found her attractive. J.R. used to call her hideous."

"What a horrible thing to say! I've never met him, but I don't like your brother. How dare he judge someone on the way she looks."

"I know, right? While I was servin' the apprenticeship, Maddie moved to Charlotte to attend Cosmetology school. After graduation, she came home, plannin' on opening her own business. But she sure didn't look like she used to."

They paused when the waiter stopped by to refill their glasses and check on their meal.

Miss Lexi's voice was softer when she spoke. "How had she changed?"

"She now looked like a million bucks. Her figure filled out and while she was in the big city, she got dental work. She's definitely the best-looking cowgirl in our town. All my friends were jealous."

"How'd that make you feel?"

Clifton rubbed his hand across his face as he remembered. "Her looks didn't mean nothing to me. Believe it or not, I fell in love with her heart, not how she looked. Oh, I was happy she'd changed, just because it made her feel better about herself. However, looks alone couldn't a never have made me love her more. I do gotta admit it though, she sure does turn every head when she walks into a room."

Miss Lexi's eyes reflected a sadness to them. "What happened, Cliff?"

"J.R.—that's what. I was told his jaw dropped to the floor when he caught sight a her again. I guess that's when he decided she should belong to him, not me. Another competition between us. The lowlife inserted himself into her world. When she decided to open her own shop, my big brother benevolently offered her both legal and financial assistance. Being the phony J.R. is, he wooed her as well. I warned

Maddie what he was like, but she told me I got it all wrong. She thought J.R. was only helping because we were 'all gonna be a big family one day'."

"He stole her away from you, didn't he?"

"I imagine his seemingly limitless wealth, coupled with the crap he fed her, contributed to her feelings for him. I finally decided to put an end to it, so that's when I asked Maddie to marry me. Know what she told me?"

"If this is too painful, you don't have to share this."

"No. Ma'am, I want you to know the truth about who I am... and why I act the way I do. You're some kind of special in my eyes. I'm telling you this so there ain't no secrets between us."

"Sorry. Please continue. What did Maddie reply?"

He swallowed hard before continuing. "She said... she told me... well, Maddie declared she couldn't give me an answer right then and there." Clifton hesitated.

"Why?"

"Maddie said she was in love with both of us and didn't know how to answer. Couldn't decide which one of us she should choose. Well, I did it for her. I told her I'd settle for nothing less than a girl who loves me—and only me. I couldn't care less if we had any money or a big house or lots of things. I said what I really wanted was a relationship that stands the test of time. In other words, it had to be all or nothing."

"How did she react to that?" Miss Lexi's eyes seemed wet. She now held both his hands, very tightly.

"She didn't say squat, but walked out of the restaurant. Less than a week later, I heard she moved in with my scumbag brother. It took him no time at all to start spreading rumors about 'the real reason' Maddie left me. Lies about things I'd never, ever say or do to a real lady. So, I stopped by to pay him a visit and say farewell the night I headed out of town. He sure looked surprised when I knocked him on his butt. I'm sure he filed an arrest warrant for assault before I even got my truck started. Luckily, the sheriff and the local judge have known both of us for years, so they probably dragged their feet until I left town."

"I don't know what to say."

"You don't be needin' to say anything. But I reckoned ya oughta know before..."

Miss Lexi's eyes opened widely. "Before what?"

Clifton paused briefly before replying. He could feel the warmth in his cheeks. "Before I ask you out again. And if the answer is no, I'll understand."

Miss Lexi squeezed his fingers tightly before she released them. There seemed to be a look of wonder in her eyes.

She reached for her fork and knife, but just as quickly, set them down before once again engaging his eyes. "Hear me on this, Clifton McCallister. When you do get around to asking, the answer will be yes."

Chapter Five

L exi shifted the transmission into park before turning off the motor. After drawing in a lungful of cold, late autumn air, she headed for the sprawling building that housed the Paradise Bed and Breakfast. It was the location where her friend Tracilyn was staying while she recuperated from her leg injury.

Before Lexi could open the door, a young brunette threw it open. "Welcome to our inn. I'm Missi Rutledge, the hostess. Will you be staying with us?"

"No. I came to visit my friend Tracilyn. I believe she's boarding with you."

"That's right. She's resting in the great room. Follow me and I'll take you there."

The girl led her just down the hall to a large room dominated by a natural-stone fireplace. A roaring fire made it toasty inside.

Tracilyn was sitting in a wheelchair talking to a thin woman with jet-black hair. The woman smiled at Lexi and two dimples appeared on her face—one on the right cheek and a second on her chin. She offered her hand.

"Hi, I'm Ellie Campbell."

"Lexi Staples. Pleased to meet you." Lexi shifted her gaze to Tracilyn. "Hey, Trace. I stopped by to say hello, but didn't know you had company. I'll leave now. I simply wanted to say hi."

The dark-haired lady quickly stood. "Please don't go. I really stopped by to talk with Missi. She manages this place for me and we were planning on catching up." Lexi caught the smile that Ellie Campbell offered the young hostess. "I wanted to go over some ideas on decorating the B & B for Christmas."

With that, both the young brunette and the darker haired lady left, leaving Tracilyn and Lexi alone before the roaring fire.

The older woman reached for Lexi's hands. "It's so good to see you again. I missed you, Lexi. Thanks for dropping by."

Now that she was here, the atmosphere wasn't quite as strained as Lexi had expected. After all, the woman seated across from her had been the reason why Lexi had broken up with Christian.

"This is what friends do. Tell me how you're feeling and how your daughter is doing. I missed seeing the two of you at volleyball."

The comment brought a light smile to her friend's face. "After my embarrassing debacle, I'm fairly certain I'll never set foot on a volleyball court again. Even when I can someday." Tracilyn extracted an electronic device from her pocket and then displayed recent photos of her daughter's baby boy.

Conversation about Tracilyn's family occupied their time for a while, until Ms. Campbell stuck her head in the room and said farewell. Within seconds, the hostess brought them both hot tea and a slice of egg custard pie before once again departing.

Lexi consumed the filling, but allowed the crust to remain. "That pie was tasty."

"I know. Missi's mother is a baker and sends stuff over all the time. I'd be surprised if I don't gain thirty pounds while staying here."

An awkward silence followed. Lexi broke it. "How's Christian these days?"

"I don't know. Aren't you two still together?"

"No. We broke up a couple of weeks ago." Saying that phrase wasn't as hard as Lexi had anticipated. "I'm surprised he's not with you."

"Am I the reason you two parted ways?"

"That's not important. You see, no matter what he said, I could sense Chris cared for you in a way he'd never been able to feel for me. The man loves you, Traci."

The other woman shook her head. "No, that's not true and it wouldn't matter if he did. I refuse to be what comes between people I care about. Maybe the two of you could reconcile and get back together?"

"You and I are not going to argue about this. I want to be with someone who wants me and only me. Chris never got over you. That's the real reason I broke up with him."

Tracilyn's face was red. "Lexi, I'm sorry. I never meant for this to happen."

Lexi offered what she hoped was an encouraging smile. "A good friend of mine told me that everything happens for a reason." Lexi allowed her voice to change so she could mimic Clifton's southern drawl. "He says that the good Lord plans our lives that way. My friend also said that in most cases, when God takes one thing away, He replaces it with something better."

Tracilyn gazed at her for a few seconds. "Who is this friend? Are you hanging out with a philosopher these days?"

Lexi's cheeks felt warm. "No. He's just a plain, old country boy. Want to see his picture?"

Tracilyn nodded. Lexi pulled out her phone. "This is Clifton Alexander McCallister."

"Wait. I *know* this man. He was at volleyball, wasn't he?"

"Yep."

"And he has a charming Southern accent if I remember."

Lexi knew she had to be beaming. "That he does."

"Wait until I tell my daughter. She's mentioned him to me several times."

"In a good way, I hope."

"Of course. Perhaps now she'll return to volleyball."

Lexi took a sip of the tea. "Why did she quit coming?"

"Because she comes over to spend her Monday evenings with me. My girl always brings the baby and most times her boyfriend tags along. I think she does that so I won't think about missing your games."

"I'm glad the two of you are bonding like you are. I remember when we first met, you and your daughter were estranged."

"We were, but now, it's as if we're not just mother and daughter, but best friends."

"Yeah. I love it when the good guys win." Lexi smiled at her friend.

Tracilyn nodded and looked at Lexi's cell. "Not changing the subject, but... just how close are you and this Clifton guy becoming?"

"Well, he took me home and introduced me to Grandma."

"He did what? Introduced you to his family? Already?"

"Not exactly. Grandma is his dog, an old coonhound."

Tracilyn laughed. "And how did that go?"

"Well, Cliff is a little disappointed."

"Oh, I'm sorry. What happened?"

"How did Cliff put it? 'Grandma took to me like a fly to honey'. When I go over, Grandma licks my hand, wags her tail and parks herself at my feet. Cliff calls her *my* dog."

"How often do you two get together?"

Lexi's face heated. "We've seen each other every day since our first date. I'm lucky. Cliff's a great guy."

"I'm happy for you."

"Thanks. Now all we have to do is get you and Christian back together."

Her friend shook her head. "I'm afraid that will never happen."

"Oh ye of little faith. Look how God turned my life from dismal to euphoria."

"Yeah, but you're the great Lexi Staples."

"What's that supposed to mean?"

"Come on, you have a way of spreading happiness everywhere you go."

"I do?"

"Of course. You're a stream of sunshine for the world. I mean, look how many people you've touched with your volleyball league."

"Aww, stop it. It's nothing, really."

Tracilyn reached over to pat Lexi's arm. "You're wrong. You have a kind heart, Lexi. I bet God even has a nickname for you."

Lexi laughed. "And what would that be?"

"Well, since your presence is like a ray of sunlight on a cloudy day, I might know what He calls you."

"This ought to be good. What are you thinking?"

"His Sunbeam."

Chapter Six

T here was no possible way any man could feel happier than Clifton did when he was with Miss Lexi. In the five weeks since she'd locked her keys in the Kia, they'd seen each other every day. But that was going to change shortly. Miss Lexi was heading west to Colorado to spend Thanksgiving with her folks. They were running around today, getting gifts for her to take out west to her family. Their day began with a trip to Kitchen Kettle for a load of jellies and jams, followed by a visit to Good's Store for practical home items one could not buy way out there. This was the final stop before taking in a hockey game at the Giant Center in Hershey later that evening.

Clifton whipped the F-150 into an empty space in the parking lot. Quickly dismounting, he headed around to open the door for the blonde lady.

After she reached the ground, they headed for the building. A growling noise and screams filled the air.

"Is that a rollercoaster I hear? I used to love ridin' the ones at Six Flags in Charlotte."

"I believe that's the one they call the 'Great Bear'. Haven't you ever been to Hershey Park?"

"Nope."

"We'll have to go sometime. My students said they keep some of the rides open for the holidays. Maybe when I get back after Thanksgiving we can go."

"I'd like that. I gotta tell you, Lexi, I'm going to miss you next weekend."

Miss Lexi squeezed his hand. "I'll only be gone for five days."

"Which will seem like forever. So, what is this place?"

She turned to face him. "I assume you've never been to Chocolate World, either?" The beautiful lady winked at him. He shook his head. "Then, follow me and I'll reveal the secrets behind Milton Hershey's world-famous milk chocolate making process."

With Clifton in tow, Miss Lexi led him to the Chocolate World tour, which explained how the chocolatey snacks are crafted. Near the end of the tour, an automatic camera captured the images of the people in the ride. The pair stopped to see how their photograph came out.

Lexi tapped his arm. "Look. There we are, over there on the third monitor."

Clifton was captivated by the image and purchased a photo package. After exiting the tour ride, they hit the store. Three shopping bags of candy and a major hit to Lexi's credit card later, the pair shuffled to the refreshment center. Without a spoken word, they both gravitated to the stand offering iced delights.

Miss Lexi squeezed his hand. "What are you hungry for?"

"Probably a chocolate shake. How about you?"

"That was my first choice as well. My second is the strawberry ice cream sundae. Do you like that flavor?"

"I reckon I do."

A certain sparkle seemed to be lighting her blue eyes. "Do you mind ordering while I find a table?"

Because of the crowd, it was a while before Clifton turned from the pickup counter with the delicacies. He searched the crowd, looking for Miss Lexi. When his eyes finally settled on her face, Clifton noted something remarkable. It was as if there was a spotlight shining down from Heaven, lighting her face. That captivating smile drew him in as he approached.

"Here you go, ma'am." He sat next to her.

"Mind if I give thanks?"

"Please do."

Miss Lexi reached for and took his hand. "Gracious Father, we thank You for our many blessings. We appreciate the host of things You provide for us, such as the nourishment of food we're about to enjoy." The lady hesitated for a moment. "We also thank You for this relationship, for introducing us to each other. Not a thing happens that You haven't planned and designed to be. Please open our hearts and help us follow the desire You have for us. Thank You for bringing us together as such close friends. Amen."

"That was beautiful. Thank you." While they frequently said grace before each meal, her prayer that day felt different. Clifton's heart was in his throat. *Am I reading too much here?*

Miss Lexi smiled. "Mind if I sample your shake?"

"No, please help yourself."

"In return, please have some of my sundae." He watched as she took a small spoonful of her light, pink ice cream and then dipped it in his shake. Even more surprising was when she offered it to him. "Want a taste?"

"Wait a second." Clifton used his spoon and did the exact same thing Miss Lexi had done. With a full spoon of the cold treat waiting outside her lips, he smiled. "I'm ready, now."

Simultaneously, they fed each other. But it wasn't the taste of the mixture that made him feel good—instead, it was the rapidly-growing feeling in his chest. The one he'd been avoiding. A vulnerability Clifton had vowed he'd never allow again.

When the snacks were gone, they sat looking into each other's eyes.

He broke the silence. "I know you'll be busy with your family and everything, but would you mind if I called you, like every day?"

Miss Lexi's face seemed radiant. "How do you feel about me?"

"I think you know."

"We're close, but I don't want to jump to conclusions. Please tell me, Cliff."

"All right." Clifton swallowed hard before continuing. "I think I love you."

Miss Lexi's cheeks were immediately pink. "You're not just saying that to make me feel good, are you?" He shook his head. "Are you sure?"

"Nope—to just saying it to make you happy. I've felt like this for a while, but now that I actually confessed it out loud, I'm certain. I love you, Lexi Staples." He kissed her fingertips.

He picked up on the slight change in her expression—one he'd noted before. She got this look every time she joked with him.

"I'm sorry, Clifton, but the answer will have to be 'no'."

Wait. Was she teasing or being serious? "To which question?"

"The one about calling me every day."

"Why? Don't you want me to call at all?"

He could detect her effort—one where she was suppressing her laughter. "I find calling me every day will be... umm... unnecessary."

Two can play this game. "What do you have against phone calls? Does the high elevation affect your reception or somethin'?"

"Why would you place a call when you simply have to look beside you?"

"I'm not following you, ma'am."

Miss Lexi touched his face with the fingers of both hands. "I want you by my side, Cliff. Come home with me. I want to introduce you to my family."

Chapter Seven

C lifton lifted the last suitcase from the luggage carousel. The bag was filled with the gifts Miss Lexi had brought home. He almost lost his grip on the handle because his hands were wet from sweat. *Don't think I've ever been this nervous.*

In just a few minutes, they had everything packed in the rental. Lexi navigated the SUV out of the airport and onto the freeway. Clifton was captivated by the snow-covered mountains in the distance.

"You lived up in those hills?"

"I used to. But now I live in good old Pennsylvania."

"Wow. Never seen nothin' quite like that."

"I thought the South had everything. Don't you have mountains in South Carolina?" How Miss Lexi loved to tease him.

"Out in the northwest corner of the state we got some, but they ain't nothin' like these. Look at all that snow."

"I hope you packed a heavy coat, because I plan on hiking some snowy trails. I want to share my love of the outdoors with you this weekend, unless it's too chilly for a guy like you. Wait, have you ever actually seen snow?"

"I most assuredly did. I 'member the terrible flurry storm of '21. It lasted ten minutes."

They both laughed. "You and your crazy sense of humor. Are you happy you came?"

He touched her arm. She shot a smile his way. "Yes. Thank you, ma'am."

"For what?"

"Mainly for bein' so kind to me. Gotta tell you— I'm getting used to this."

"Good. We'll be home in about an hour. Want a refresher on the family?"

The miles slipped away as Miss Lexi filled the sport utility with stories and descriptions of the Staples clan. Being raised in the South, Clifton was used to family being quite important. Like his had been to him... before J.R. spoiled everything.

They stopped in front of what he guessed could be called a Swiss chalet. A huge wooden deck protruded off onto the left side of the building, offering a scenic overlook of the mountains. While a roof supported by massive beams covered some of the viewing area, snow lay heavy on the exposed deck railings. Scattered pine trees sported a blanket of frozen white precipitation, giving him the impression that he was standing in a picture from a holiday card.

"Are you ready to meet my family?" Miss Lexi's words brought him back to the here and now.

"Reckon I'm as ready as I'll ever be." Clifton carried the two heaviest pieces of luggage as he followed the beautiful girl.

Even the door at the back of the house was decorated with a spray of holly. Before he could take it in, the dark oak covering flew open. A pretty lady greeted him with a smile and then pulled Miss Lexi into her arms.

That must be her mama.

A tall, muscular man extended his hand and introductions began. Clifton had just met his girl's parents, but when they moved inside, a large group of people waited. Clifton's lips dried when his gaze fell on a man standing in the back—a man Clifton had run into before.

***

Lexi picked up on the stiffness of Clifton's reaction. *What's that about?* She held his hand and presented her friend to the family. It was great to see them all, especially her grandma. She was nearly finished with the introductions when her eyes fell onto a face she hadn't seen in years.

"Pat O'Reilly? Is that really you?"

The tall man standing in the back of the group nodded. "In the flesh." His words were accented differently than she remembered. He swept her into his arms and warmly kissed her lips. "I missed you, Lexi."

It took a few seconds, but Lexi finally wriggled out of the man's arms. She knew her cheeks must be red, based on how warm they felt. "What are you doing here?"

"I traveled home for the holidays, specifically taking a chance you just might be here. I missed you very much, Lexi. I can't look at a Rocky Mountain horizon without thinking of you. I needed to see you. We had some good times, didn't we?"

"I guess so, years ago." Lexi could feel Clifton's eyes on her. She reached for her boyfriend's hand and was shocked by how cold it was. "Cliff, I'd like to introduce you to—"

Her friend yanked his hand away and then cut her off. "We've already met."

"You have?" Lexi searched Clifton's face. "What's wrong?"

"Nothin'. Now, if you'll excuse me, I think I need some fresh air." With that, her boyfriend stepped outside, closing the heavy oak door behind him.

"Is something the matter?" Lexi turned to find her father by her side.

"I don't know." She faced Pat. "Cliff said you two have met before?"

A charming, Irish smile awaited her. "Oh, we've run into each other a couple of times, but I have no idea why he stormed out like that."

"How is it possible you two know each other?"

"As you probably remember, I live in Charlotte, North Carolina. It's not that far away from where Cliff and his family live. The entire South is like a big neighborhood. Everyone simply knows everybody."

It seemed to Lexi that Pat was keeping something from her. "I still don't understand why Cliff reacted that way to your presence."

"I'm not sure, Lexi. Maybe it's because he was startled I was here... and okay, let's put all the cards on the table. I'm afraid to tell you the true reason. Most likely, he's scared I would spill what I know about him."

"And what would that be?"

"His temper, Lexi. That man has a reputation as a hot head. I've heard rumors suggesting he physically abused his girlfriend and that's why he had to leave South Carolina in such a hurry."

Chapter Eight

I t was freezing outside. In his haste to get away from Mr. Pat O'Reilly, Clifton had forgotten to bring along his coat. The crisp and clear evening revealed a billion stars overhead, but he imagined it couldn't be any colder in deep space that it was right here. His breath hung like a vapor cloud in front of him. *What is the possibility* he *would be here?* Clifton trembled in the frigid Colorado night.

High above the mountains, the lights of an airliner pulsed as the flight path took it east. *Wish I was on that plane.* With each passing minute that he stood alone in the night, his hope for a future with Miss Lexi faded... just like the lights of the plane above.

Shivering started, mildly at first, then violently. He had no option. *I need to go back inside and grab my jacket to leave, after I warm up.*

Breaking down, he reentered, greedily soaking up the warmth inside. Much to his surprise, the room was empty. From somewhere deep inside the structure, he heard his girl's voice and then her laughter. It was over. Pat O'Reilly had buffaloed Miss Lexi—and she fell for him, hook, line and sinker.

Clifton slipped on his coat and sank into an easy chair. Silently, he began to collect his thoughts and words. Perhaps the Staples would be kind enough to provide the number for a service that would take him back to the airport. If not, he'd hitchhike. In either case, it was time for him to go.

A honking horn interrupted Clifton's thought. His mouth dropped open. *Did they already call a ride to take me away?* Footsteps echoed along the hardwood floors of the hallway. His heart was in his throat when Miss Lexi turned the corner. In confusion, he noted the tray she carried held two steaming cups of liquid.

"Glad you came back in. It can get downright chilly out there at night." She sat across from him and offered a mug. "Brought you some hot chocolate to warm you up."

"Thanks."

They stared at each other until the silence seemed unbearable. Luckily, Miss Lexi broke it. "How do you know Patrick?"

"I'm sure he filled you in."

"He had a few things to say, but then, he always did."

"Yeah. He would."

"Okay, but I'd like to hear it from you. I don't want to judge someone I care about on another's testimony."

"Fine. I met Mr. O'Reilly 'bout a year ago. My brother was looking to expand his practice and the two hooked up. I thought the man was nice at first, but then when those two started working together, well, I found out he wasn't as genuine as he first appeared to be."

Lexi took a sip of her drink. She grabbed a tissue and quickly wiped away the thin chocolate residue from her lips. "In what way?"

"He lied to Maddie to help drive a wedge between us, just so J.R. could get his hooks into my girl. Maddie wanted to see some Kenny Chesney concert up in Charlotte. I bought tickets so I could take her, plannin' on surprising my girl. Two nights before the event, they disappeared from my room."

"How did Pat play into this? Are you inferring he took them?"

"Naw, but he was there the night it all came to a head. Maddie was over for dinner. I excused myself to go grab the passes, but they were gone from where I had them on my dresser. I came back downstairs and couldn't believe my eyes. Maddie was jumping up and down, when she wasn't hugging my brother. In her hands were the ticket stubs. J.R. had given them to her, and of course, took credit for getting them."

"But wait, you had proof you purchased them, right? You bought the tickets on a credit card, I imagine."

Clifton shook his head. "Nope. Paid cash."

"Did you try to explain it to her?"

"I called my brother a liar, but your friend jumped right in there and confirmed J.R.'s version. Said he'd even picked up the tickets himself in Charlotte for J.R., since he lived there."

Lexi hesitated. "Is there more you're not telling me? Specifically, concerning Madelaine?"

Clifton studied the floor. "I lost my cool. I yanked those stupid things from her hand and tore the tickets to shreds. My anger scared her. That was kinda the beginning of the end. Of course, my brother had connections and got Maddie backstage passes not only for the show, but to meet Kenny Chesney in person."

Miss Lexi was silent for a few moments. "Did you ever get physical with Madelaine?"

Clifton began to see red. He'd heard talk that J.R. and Pat O'Reilly claimed he'd tried to strike Maddie, saying they had saved her from harm. "If you have to ask, *ma'am,* then you never once knew me."

"But I am asking. I want to hear *you* tell me the truth."

"Lexi, my mama taught me never to hit no girl for no reason at all. I wouldn't do that to one I didn't like, so I most assuredly wouldn't a ever raised a finger against someone I used to love."

Those beautiful blue eyes on Miss Lexi's face were troubled.

"Know what? I'm thinkin' it's time for me to say goodbye."

"Why? Because it's uncomfortable talking about this issue? Our discussion is part of the process of getting to a resolution. Is that what's the matter?"

"No. I'm thinkin' you believe the lies that Pat O'Reilly guy told you."

She seemed to recoil and her cheeks turned pink. "If that's what you believe, then maybe it's *you* who doesn't really know me."

"Come again?"

"I am not just another pretty face. I have a brain and know how to use it. I draw my own conclusions." She paused.

"And what would they be?"

"Two things—first, people change over time. But more importantly, actions speak louder than words."

Clifton was confused. "What does that mean?"

"Pat's no longer here, but you are."

"And?"

"I asked him to leave. But I want you to stay. Will you?"

**

Lexi stared at Pat. "Cliff hit a girl?"

His right eye twitched slightly before he responded. Pat gazed at her. She remembered not only seeing that involuntary reaction before, but knew exactly what it meant when it happened. "That is what you were suggesting, weren't you?"

He still didn't reply, but instead nodded slightly.

"Let's back up. How do you know Cliff?"

"Like I mentioned, it's all one big neighborhood below the Mason-Dixon line."

He was grandstanding because of the audience—Lexi's family. *I need to shut this down.* "Let's head into the kitchen where we can talk—in private."

A quick glance in her mother's direction sealed the deal. The older lady turned to the family. "I think we'd be more comfortable in the living room. Let's get warm by the fire."

While her family departed for the large room with the stone hearth, Lexi led Pat into the kitchen. The man had a funny smile on his face.

"I haven't been in here for years. I do believe you kissed me for the first time right... about... here. And then..." He had inched closer and moved to embrace her.

Lexi backed away. "Stop it, right now. How do you know Cliff?"

He sighed as he backed away. "His brother and I have business dealings."

She nodded. "That's right, I forgot you were an attorney. Public defender, if I remember correctly."

"There was no money in that."

"And the last time we spoke, you were thinking about moving over to the District Attorney's office, so you could get justice for victims."

"Again, that doesn't pay well enough."

It began to make sense to Lexi. *Money—the root of all evil.* "But let me guess—the personal injury realm is quite exclusive and financially rewarding, isn't it?"

He smiled, revealing brilliant white-capped teeth. "There are certain incentives, but helping those wronged by the actions of others is why I changed practices. I get justice for my clients."

Lexi laughed, loudly. "I bet you do, while lining your own pockets. I'd almost forgotten why we broke up."

The smile disappeared. "What are you inferring?"

"You were always self-centered. I thought when you took a job defending others, you might have changed. But now, I can see you've returned to your roots. That is, your true colors are showing."

"Taking on those who have wronged others has more than a financial component. There's a certain satisfaction—"

Lexi threw her hands in front of her. "Puh-lease—stop it. Know what? I think it's time for you to leave."

Pat stared at her as if in disbelief. "Why? I came all the way back here to see you again. After all, we have a future together." He reached for her hand.

"You haven't really changed. You tried to force yourself into my life years ago and that didn't work. Guess what? It surely won't now. Get out."

"And leave you with a man who hit his girlfriend?"

"You mean 'allegedly'. Nice try, but I know Cliff too well to believe that. Leave. Get out of my house."

"But Lexi..." He again moved as if to hold her.

"Touch me again and I'll make you regret it for the rest of your miserable existence. Goodbye."

His expression changed and he hissed the word through clenched teeth. "Fine."

Lexi led him to the front door and watched as Pat climbed into his car. She wasn't surprised when he pointed his ride out of the drive, pausing only to honk the horn and send a rude gesture her way.

Her thoughts were now focused on the man at the rear of the house—the real victim in Pat's tirade. She quickly made hot chocolate and returned to where she'd left Clifton. She needed to hear his side of the story.

After listening, she said, "I want you to stay. Will you?"

He harumphed and shook his head. "Why?"

"Because we traveled all this way to meet my family."

"After being publicly humiliated and, if I heard you right, accused of roughing up a lady, you want me to stay?"

"Yes."

"Again, why? I'm sure your family has already formed their opinions of me."

Lexi paused before responding. "I mean no offense by this, but my family is different than most. We try our best to act like God would want us to. There aren't any hidden agendas or evil under-currents." Lexi studied her cup for a moment. "May I ask a question?"

A frown still covered his face and Lexi felt for him. "Of course."

"Am I like Maddie? I mean, do you think I could be fooled by cleverly cloaked words or plots?"

"No, ma'am."

"Why not?"

"Because you are genuinely kind. You wear your heart on your sleeve and always make people feel good. And besides, you're way too smart to have someone pull the wool over your eyes."

"Where do you think I got that from?"

"Most likely, good upbringing, I reckon."

She snickered. "You've got that right. So, here's your take-away. Don't judge my family before you get a chance to know them, okay?"

"Understood. I'm sorry."

"No apologies needed." She stood and offered her hand. "It's time to meet my family. They're all waiting in the living room."

"For what?"

"To get to know the man I love."

Chapter Nine

C lifton couldn't believe his good fortune in finding Miss Lexi. He'd never met anyone who was as honest or caring as this lady. After the debacle involving Pat O'Reilly and how the man tried to discredit Clifton in front of the Staples clan, Miss Lexi and her family made Clifton feel welcome. Almost as if he was fully accepted into her family.

Since their return, the pair had become inseparable. Evenings and nights were spent together, although they slept in separate rooms. Because of his old coonhound, the two usually stayed at Clifton's apartment. Clifton gave Miss Lexi his bed while he snoozed on the couch. And of course, his canine, Grandma, camped out on top of the covers so the dog could be close to her new best friend.

On the last Monday before Christmas, the weekly volleyball game had just finished. As usual, he and Miss Lexi were the last ones there, cleaning up. Clifton couldn't help notice not only Lexi's smile, but how his girl was humming to herself.

"Whatcha singing?"

A tired smile adorned her face. "Christmas carols. I love this time of year."

"Me, too. Which one has your fancy this evening?"

"The one that has the line, 'there's no place like home for the holidays'."

"Yeah, I like that one too. Do you wish you were heading home to the Rockies for Christmas?"

Miss Lexi set down the broom and walked until she stood before him. Taking his hands, she searched his face.

"Not really. I was thinking about you and your family. Wouldn't you like to see them over the holidays?"

"I would, but there's a problem—a big one. My brother and Maddie will be there. I can do without the drama."

"What about the rest of the family?"

"It would be good to see Mama and my sisters. Both Pam and Sue Ellen have little kids and they are what truly makes the season magical."

She was silent as she studied him. Her words were softly spoken when delivered. "Don't let him ruin your life or steal your joy."

"Nonsense. *You* are my joy, Lexi."

"As you are mine. The decision is up to you, but if you want to go home, I'll gladly offer to tag along. You know, to protect you and stuff."

Clifton noted the slight change of expression on the lady's face. He knew it meant she was about to tease him.

"Okay, let me have it. Why the smile?"

"Is it wrong to be happy?"

"When y'all is about to pick on me, it might be. What were you goin' to say?"

"Oh, you know. I was just wondering if maybe you were like, you know, ashamed of me or something, and that was the reason you're not returning home."

"What in the blazes? Why are you talkin' so funny?"

"Maybe it's because you're embarrassed by the way I act or look."

"Now wait one cotton-pickin' minute, I could never be ashamed of you. You are beautiful and act kinda like how I expect an angel would." Clifton stopped when he heard her giggle.

Miss Lexi not only knew what she was doing, but had figured exactly how he would react. The lady had offered bait, and like a big-mouthed bass, he swallowed the entire hook, line and sinker. Not only that, he'd run with it toward the deepest hole in the lake.

"So, you kind of like me, huh?"

Two can play this game. "Nope—not at all, least no more." He noted the look of worried surprise in his girl's eyes.

"What? Really?"

He quickly scooped her into his arms. "Come on, Lexi. It's more than just liking you, girl. A whole lot more. I hope you know it by now. I am hopelessly in love with you."

***

"Are we there yet?" She laughed when he shot her a sideways glance. "Seriously, how much farther is it?" Lexi released Clifton's hand and stretched.

The three of them were tired after being on the road for almost eight hours. The two humans had split the driving miles while Grandma slept on the seat between them, head resting on Lexi's lap whether the lady was in the passenger or driver's seat.

"We've got about three miles to go before we get to Mama's house. What do you think of my hometown, Liberty Hills?"

"Well, it's certainly quaint."

"The area ain't nothing at all like Lancaster County, is it?"

"I kind of like the openness. Less hustle and bustle, you know?"

"And the thirty to one cow-to-people ratio helps, huh?"

"You've got me there. I've always been fond of cows... and other animals." She looked at the coonhound. "Right, sweetie?" As if on cue, Grandma—with her eyes still closed—slowly wagged her tail, slapping Clifton's arm. Lexi couldn't help but laugh.

"This here's the road I was raised on." Clifton slowed and turned left onto a dirt lane.

Lexi wasn't impressed. They passed an old double-wide trailer with tattered blue tarps covering the roof. At least two generations of rotting Ford pickups rested on concrete blocks in the front yard while waiting for rust to totally consume them. The lawn surrounding the structure was full of weeds and the wooden porch sagged almost to the ground. In fact, the entire place was run-down, except for a very new-looking carport anchored next to the living quarters. Parked underneath was a shiny, sparkling clean pickup with big mud tires, a fog light rack and a tonneau cover.

Her boyfriend caught her gaze. "I see Billy Johnson bought himself a new ride. Kind of rad, ain't it?"

"Why would he do that? The house needs work. Shouldn't that be his priority?"

Clifton laughed. "Welcome to the South. We's an unusual bunch... to you Yankees."

"I don't know about the rest of the people here, but a clown is what you are."

Coming up on the right were a number of park trailers, haphazardly placed on a grassy lot as if they had been thrown there. A bunch of kids were playing outside.

As the truck approached, the children ran to the road and waved. Some even called out Clifton's name.

"Is that your family?"

"Naw, just the neighbor kids." Clifton hesitated. "You do know why the trailer park is there, don't you?"

"To provide housing for low-income families?"

"No, that'd be a second benefit. The trailers are..." Clifton released the wheel and used his fingers to signify quotation marks. "...tornado bait."

"What?"

"In case there's a twister, we figure it'll head for the trailer park first and leave the real houses be."

She couldn't help but smile at Clifton's sense of humor. "I'd forgotten you were a redneck."

"Hey, don't be a hater, but here's your sign. You can take the boy out of the country, but not the country outta the boy. Luckily, I got you to help me navigate that so-called civilized world up north, you know, above the Mason-Dixon line."

Rounding a bend in the road, a huge, white house appeared. In direct contrast to what Lexi had previously observed with others in the area, this home and the surrounding buildings were well maintained. The yard appeared freshly mowed and Lexi quickly noted the absence of fallen leaves. It was obvious the owner took pride in the place.

"Here's where I grew up, Lexi. Welcome to my mama's house."

Clifton turned the truck onto a graveled path and dropped it in park. Before the motor could stop spinning, the front door flew open and a mass of people poured onto the porch.

When he reached for the door handle, Lexi grabbed his arm. "Were you this nervous when you came to meet my parents?"

The man seemed to focus his full attention on Lexi. "Much worse, I believe. My wish for today is that I can be as supporting to you as you were to me." He leaned across and kissed her cheek.

The throng had now surrounded the truck. Clifton stepped out and was engulfed in the arms of a white-haired lady. Grandma abandoned Lexi, tail wagging as she jumped to the lawn. The passel of kids took turns petting her.

Then, everyone's attention turned to Lexi. Swallowing hard, she slid across the seat. Clifton grasped Lexi by the hips and gently placed her on solid ground. All eyes were on her.

"Mama, everybody, I'd like you all to meet Miss Lexi Staples. She's my girlfriend. Lexi, this is my mama."

Extending her hand toward the older woman, Lexi offered what she hoped was a genuine smile.

Clifton's mother ignored Lexi's outstretched limb, and instead pulled Lexi into a tight embrace. "Family don't shake hands down here, honey—we hug. I am so pleased to meet you. Welcome to our home."

Chapter Ten

L exi climbed up in the cab. Clifton followed closely behind her. Without being asked, Grandma leapt onto Clifton's lap before parking herself between the two adults.

Her man winked before starting his Ford. "Ain't had a chance to talk to you since we got here. How you holdin' up?"

"To be honest, it's been a whirlwind. Your mother and sisters are really kind. Their children are not only well-mannered, they're well behaved. And in case you didn't know, they missed you."

"I felt like that, too, but I'm never moving back."

Lexi smiled at his comment. "That's a shame. I was thinking how nice it would be to live down here. We could have family get-togethers, picnics..."

"I don't know if you'd feel the same after my brother-in-law, Ashford, took you giggin' frogs. That's where he took Sue Ellen on their first date. In case you didn't know it, he's kind of fond of you."

Her cheeks warmed. "I know. I caught a bit of the heated conversation between Ashford and his wife, Sue Ellen. She told him if he turned sweet on me, he better get used to sleeping in the doghouse or she might spear him, whatever that meant."

"Don't worry none about him. Ash does like to look at purty girls, but he's totally devoted to my sister. Well, mostly." He squeezed her hand. "Would you really want to move down here?"

"It depends."

"On?"

"Where you are. If you stay in Pennsylvania, that's where you'll find me. But if you move here, well..."

"Don't worry about that, darlin'. I don't plan on ever coming back."

"Why not?"

"You'll meet the reason in a few minutes."

She nodded. "When your mom told me about tonight, it did seem like a strange tradition. A Christmas Eve cruise on the lake?"

"It started when my lawyer brother passed the bar and was given that huge boat as a payment for a case. J.R. always loved Lake Wateree. He and I used to fish those waters for bass and catfish when I was a kid. Back when we got along."

"Wateree—that's kind of a funny name. Do you know the origin?"

"Yep, it was named for the Native American Indian tribe that lived in the area, back before us rednecks inherited the earth." Clifton lifted the turn signal. "We're almost here."

Just beyond a bend in the road was a parking area. At the end of a pier sat a large pontoon boat, decorated with multi-colored lights. Smoke was rising from a grill at the rear of the vessel.

"I see the rest of the family's here already."

"Well, my older brother is the favored son." He slapped the truck in park and turned off the motor.

Lexi softly touched his arm. "Not to me. I love you, Cliff. If things get out of hand, lean on me. I'll always be in your corner."

"Thanks, Lexi." He swallowed hard and shifted in the seat. "It's not J.R. that bothers me. I know Maddie will be on board. Like I told you, I used to love her. This is gonna be tough."

"All the more reason for me to be here."

"Thanks, honey." He leaned over and they softly kissed. "Let's get this over with."

Clifton popped the door and hopped out. Grandma jumped right past him, heading to the boat. The man then reached for Lexi and helped her out of the cab. Hand-in-hand, they walked down the pier to the floating party. A short ladder led the way to the deck of party central.

Lexi's feet had barely touched the solid surface when a very attractive man approached. He held a long-necked bottle in his hand.

"Well, well. Seems my younger brother finally did good." His eyes roved up and down Lexi's body as he took a swig, eventually returning his gaze to her face. "Real good. Name's John Ross, but you can call me J.R. Find a place to park it and we'll get this party under way." The older brother shot a demeaning glance at Clifton. "Cliffy knows everybody on board. Some better than most."

As J.R. walked away, Lexi turned her attention back to Clifton. "Are you all right?"

But Clifton didn't answer. Instead, his eyes were focused behind her.

Lexi swiveled to face the direction of his gaze. Her mouth almost fell open. In front of Lexi stood a dark-haired girl, perhaps the most attractive woman Lexi had ever seen. The woman could have just stepped out of a beauty magazine. But what concerned Lexi most was the way the girl's eyes focused on Clifton.

After a few seconds, she gave her attention to Lexi by extending her hand. "Hi, it's a pleasure to meet y'all. My name is Maddie Brown."

***

Clifton had forgotten how pretty Madelaine was, but that wasn't his main thought. He remembered the camaraderie over the years, long before the dental work and her physical maturation. His mind drifted back to the years together, first as best friends and then as a couple.

Miss Lexi's voice interrupted the memory as she introduced herself to his former girlfriend. "I've heard a lot about you."

Madelaine blushed. "Good things, I hope."

"Of course. Cliff is always respectful. He's both the sweetest and kindest man I've ever met."

The dark-haired girl's eyes met his. "That's somethin' we both agree on."

"Maddie, do you have everyone's order?" The male voice that had called out seemed familiar, but Clifton couldn't immediately place who it belonged to.

"Be right there." Madelaine shook her head and then extracted a tablet from her pocket. "Forgot I was the appointed waitress tonight. Would you like a burger or chicken?"

After taking their order, Madelaine headed for the back of the boat.

Clifton turned to Miss Lexi. "Thank you for being here tonight and an extra appreciation for your kind words."

"I meant them. You are special."

"What did you think of my brother?"

"I didn't get a good vibe from him, but don't worry about me. I can handle myself."

She paused. "Cliff, I know you really cared for Maddie. I can still sense something in the air between you. You remember what happened between Christian and me, that he never got over Tracilyn. That was the second time in my life I lost someone I cared about to an old love. I don't want that to happen again. Maybe the two of you should talk."

"Wait, no. Lexi, I love you."

"Good, because I love you, too. But I want to be wanted for me and only me. I won't accept a man's love if his heart isn't completely mine. It's okay. Go and talk to her."

"But I don't want to abandon you."

She smiled and Clifton knew it was genuine. Then, he noted the corners of her mouth curl a little more. "I think I'll find Ashford and let him describe in detail the art of gouging frogs."

"You mean giggin' frogs?"

"Is there a difference?" His girl winked before departing.

He watched her walk off and his heart warmed. Miss Lexi truly was a gem.

"She seems real nice."

Clifton knew who was there before he spun around. Facing Madelaine, he replied. "Miss Lexi is the most wonderful woman I ever met."

The dark-haired woman's smile seemed melancholy. "I 'member when you'd talk like that about me." Her gaze suddenly locked on him. "I know it's too late, but I wanted to say I'm sorry. I'd sure feel better if you'd forgive me."

It felt as if a giant weight had been lifted from him. "I did, a while back."

"I miss my best friend. Leaving you for your brother was so stupid. You have no idea how many times I've relived that day in my mind. I'd give everything I own to go back in time and do it over. But I can't."

"It's okay, Maddie. I guess we just weren't meant to be."

She shook her head. "I don't believe that for a second. But I see the way you and that girl look at each other. Ain't no way I'm gonna come between the two of you, no matter what I want. I'd rather die first."

"Maddie..."

"And now I'm trapped."

Trapped? The girl's choice of words puzzled him. "What do you mean?"

"Your brother loaned me money to start my business. And because of that, he acts like he owns me. I'm gettin' sick and tired of him controlling me."

"Why don't you break up with him?"

"I tried. J.R. told me that if I leave him, he'll not only take away my business, he'll sue me and have me thrown in jail."

"Bring a lawsuit against you? For what?"

"For not repayin' the money I got from him to start my business."

"How much did you borrow?"

"Twenty thousand."

"Can't you get a bank loan?"

Madelaine briefly glanced at the rear of the vessel. "I tried that, too. Boy, was he mad when he found out. He talked to the banker and they turned me down. I paid for that mistake for a long time."

Clifton felt sad for his friend. Despite them no longer being a couple, his heart went out to her.

An idea surfaced and he spoke before thinking. "What if I loaned you the money?"

"Y-you'd do that for me?"

"Of course. That's what friends are for." An ugly thought reared its head. "Just let me bounce it off Lexi first."

Madelaine jumped up and embraced him. "Thank you, Cliff. You really are the best." Her eyes met his. "I hope you know I never stopped loving you." To his utter surprise, she grabbed him behind the neck and planted her lips on his.

He quickly pushed her away. "Never do that again."

The girl's face was red. "Sorry, I don't know what came over me."

"I think I do." They both turned to find Miss Lexi standing there.

Chapter Eleven

A fter encouraging Clifton to talk it out with Madelaine, Lexi mingled with his family. It was pleasant, the way his mother and sisters accepted Lexi so readily. Despite what she'd told Clifton, she avoided Ashford for obvious reasons.

"You do look nice tonight."

Lexi spun to the owner of those words. It was J.R.

"Thanks. Being with Cliff brings out the best in me."

"Hmm. From what I've heard, you've always been pleasant, beautiful, and oh-so-appealing." His eyes once again dropped from her face.

"What you've heard? From who?"

"I understand we have a friend in common. You do remember Pat O'Reilly?"

"Unfortunately."

"We're business partners."

Speaking with J.R. made Lexi's skin crawl, as if she'd fallen into a pit of slimy snakes covered with centipedes. The thought of Pat O'Reilly added rusty nails to the feeling. "Why am I not surprised?"

"Pat told me you took my younger brother home to meet your family at Thanksgiving. Are you two serious about a relationship?"

"I love your brother."

"Good for you, but I don't see a ring on your finger." He winked. "You know, you could do *much* better."

Lexi ignored his innuendo. "I didn't see one on Maddie's either."

"Why pay for the cow when you get the milk for free?" The man laughed. "Pat did say you were sharp—perhaps the smartest woman he'd ever met."

"When I see him again, I'll thank him for saying that."

"Then just walk to the rear of the boat. Pat's tending the grill."

Lexi glanced to the back of the pontoon. And sure enough, Pat O'Reilly was standing there, a meat spatula in one hand and a beer in the other. But he wasn't watching the food. His eyes were on Lexi. When he caught her gaze, he smiled and then nodded.

Quite a different gesture than he shot my way outside my parents' house. She turned away.

"Are you watching this?"

J.R.'s voice again drew her attention and she followed his stare. At the front of the boat, Clifton and Madelaine were in deep conversation. But the thing that concerned her was the way they were holding hands. When they hugged, Lexi knew she needed to find out what was going on.

She had almost reached them when the other woman grabbed Clifton behind the head and kissed him. To his credit, her boyfriend shoved the girl away.

"Never do that again." His cheeks were pink as he hissed the words.

"Sorry, I don't know what came over me."

Lexi had trusted Clifton when he described the situation with his brother, but experiencing all the drama in living color was a different thing.

"I think I do." Lexi's words caught their attention.

"I apologize. I didn't mean to—"

"It's fine. Cliff, can we talk…" Lexi cut off the other woman, before shooting a less than trusting glance at Madelaine. "Privately?"

The pair moved to a corner of the boat. Clifton could feel the tremble in Miss Lexi's hands. Her gaze left him feeling naked.

"What just happened?"

"She tried to kiss me and I stopped her."

"No, before that. What was going on?"

He nodded. "You deserve the truth, Lexi." Clifton recapped the conversation, but stopped short of telling his girl how he'd offered helping Madelaine get a loan.

Miss Lexi studied his face. "I know there's more. What aren't you telling me?"

"I, uh, kind of offered to like, maybe help her get a loan. You know, so she can get away from J.R."

"You what?"

"I offered to help her out of her predicament. But then I told her I needed to talk it over with you first."

The girl's jaw was clenched. "You go do what you want, Cliff. I'll have no part of this. Don't you realize they're using you?"

Miss Lexi turned and walked away from him. He watched in shock as she headed to the rear of the boat. That's when he saw them. J.R. and Madelaine stood to the side, clinking their long-necked bottles together while laughing. He noted they were holding hands. And in that moment in time, Clifton knew he'd been played for a fool.

***

Lexi stood at the rail, eyes studying the night sky. The day, like her life, had been so full of promise just a few hours ago. Until once again, a man she loved betrayed her. Five years ago, she'd walked in on her boyfriend Trevon, who just happened to be holding his ex-betrothed in his arms. It happened again just a few short months ago when she discovered Christian, the man she loved, still had serious feelings for her friend Tracilyn. And now? Clifton and Madelaine. Was he no better than the rest?

She became aware of someone standing to her left. An arm slipped around her shoulder and someone pulled her into a tight embrace. A pair of lips grazed her hair, almost making her wretch. The scent of stale beer on the man's breath filled the air.

"It's okay, Lex. I knew he'd hurt you, but I'm here now. I'll make you forget he ever existed." The words were slightly slurred.

Lexi's body stiffened. "Get your hands off me, Pat. Now!"

"No, baby. Not this time. I'm never going to let you go."

"So help me! Get your filthy mitts off of me."

She tried to escape his clutches, but he was too strong. "Don't fight it. Kiss me, Lexi, just like you used to."

"You're drunk. Let me go now or I'll scream."

Pat's hand covered her mouth. "Not this time, you won't. You're mine, now."

A harsh bark was followed by a threatening growl. They both looked down to discover Grandma standing less than a few feet away. The coonhound's ears were flat and her teeth were showing.

"Get away from me, you stupid mutt."

Grandma edged closer to Pat, her growl more menacing. Lexi noted that everyone on the barge was now focused on the situation.

Pat grabbed the meat spatula from the grill and raised it over his head.

That was when Grandma made her move. The dog lurched forward and hit O'Reilly in the chest with her front paws. Pat released Lexi as he tried to regain his balance. His arms pinwheeled as he fell backwards.

Pat might have steadied himself when he landed against the railing, but Grandma continued her defense of Lexi. The dog again threw her weight against the man... and both of them went over the rail and into the black waters of Lake Wateree.

Before she could even move, Clifton's mother was there, holding Lexi. "There, there, honey child. Are you okay? Did he hurt you?"

"No. I'm sorry about this."

"Don't be. I saw the whole thing and it weren't your fault." The woman turned to her son-in-law, Ashford. "Get the dog out of the water and dry her off. It would be a shame if she caught a cold."

"What do you want to do about O'Reilly, Mama?"

"I'd like to leave him in the water for the critters, but that man's so rotten I'm not sure the gators would even touch him." Mama smiled at Lexi. "I reckon we oughta fetch him out, seeing that it's Christmas Eve and all."

A trembling hand now touched Lexi's shoulder. It belonged to Clifton. "Lexi, are you all right?"

His mother answered for her. "Where were you when this went down? I thought I taught you better than this. Like how to treat a lady proper-like. Now go back to the front of the boat and think about what you did... or rather *didn't* do. Git!"

Lexi almost laughed out loud when she caught the look on Clifton's face. He forced his jaw closed and nodded. "Yes, ma'am."

Head down, Clifton retreated.

Mama whispered in Lexi's ear. "Men! Sometimes, you gotta put them in their place. Cliff's a good boy, just misguided at times."

Misguided? Is that why he'd tried to help out Madelaine, or was it because he still loved his ex-girlfriend?

Chapter Twelve

I t was well after midnight. Lexi sat on the bed that had been Clifton's when he lived in this house. The man was now downstairs on the couch. Grandma was snuggled on the quilt, obviously resting after rescuing Lexi.

It was early Christmas morning. Lexi knew she should be sleeping, but that seemed unlikely to happen anytime soon. Perhaps it was from all the chaos on the boat or maybe the decision she was mulling over in her mind. Lexi did the only thing she could. Eyes closed, she prayed.

"God, I need your help. You know my story and how every time I fall in love, I find out my man loves somebody else more. I can't do this anymore. Please direct me to the man of Your choosing, but please, please make him a faithful man—to both You and me. I seem to be a little dense, so if You wouldn't mind, please send me a sign even I can't miss. Thanks for listening, Lord. Amen."

Lexi loved Clifton, but perhaps he really wasn't the man for her. She needed someone to cherish her enough to forsake all others.

After hours of debate, she finally gave up. Climbing under the covers, Lexi pulled the sheet up to her chin. Whether she was actually asleep or in the fog that comes before slumber, she felt Grandma stand up on the bed. The dog was staring at the window, emitting a scary, snarling noise.

Lexi quickly sat up. Earlier in the day, she had observed there was a porch roof just outside the window of the room she now occupied. Grandma's ears went flat and Lexi noted the white fangs once again appear on the dog's face.

Staring out into the night, Lexi saw a figure climb onto the roof. Her heart was in her throat. Grandma jumped off the bed, keeping herself between the window and Lexi.

Suddenly, the dog's tail started thumping. The growl had been replaced by a happy, whining noise. That's when she heard the voice, a kind of harsh, whispered string of words.

"Lexi, are you awake?"

Was that Clifton's voice?

"Lexi, it's me. Can we talk, pretty please?"

It *was* him. She walked to the window and raised the sash. "What are you doing? Come inside before you fall off the roof."

"No, I'm fine out here. I just needed to talk to you... to hear your voice. I felt that if I didn't, I'd go insane."

"You are crazy, climbing on a roof at this time of night. Well, here I am. What do you want me to say?"

"That you'll listen to me explain what happened. That's all I ask."

Immense sadness filled her chest. "Cliff, it's okay. I know you and Maddie were close. She holds a special place in your heart and she always will. That—"

"No, Lexi, that's not it at all. The reason I tried to help her wasn't affection, it was guilt. She was my best friend for years and the reason I wanted to assist her was because I thought my brother was taking advantage of her."

"He is. He basically said that to me. Something about *why buy the cow when you get the milk for free.*"

"Sounds like him, but there's something else that happened tonight. Didn't you find it strange Pat O'Reilly was here?"

"Kind of. But I just assumed he might always be here."

"Not so. J.R. has five other lawyers in his office. But O'Reilly was the only one here tonight."

That opened her eyes a bit. "Okay. I'll admit that's odd."

"Let me ask you this. I know you saw Maddie try to kiss me. How did you come to witness that?"

"I was talking to your brother and he... wait. He pointed you two out just before she attempted to kiss you."

"Um-hmm. And after you and I argued, I saw Maddie and J.R. celebrating."

She stared at Clifton in disbelief. "You're right. Now that I think back, I noted that as well. Oh goodness, we were both set up, weren't we?"

"Afraid so. I'm sorry you got pulled into the drama." Clifton briefly studied her. "We can head home in the morning, that is, if you still want to ride with me."

Something tugged at her heart, as if a hidden hand was nudging her. "Can I ask you something?"

"Of course."

"How do you feel about me?"

"I love you, Lexi. More than anything or anyone else in the world."

"But if I wanted out of this relationship, that would be okay?"

"No, it would never be tolerable, at least to me. But if that's what you really wanted, I'd lie and tell you it was fine."

"Why?"

"Because your happiness will always be more important than mine. Do you want us to end?"

Her heart pushed her onward. "When you think of us, how do you picture me?"

He hesitated for a second or two. "It's like my entire world is black and white, until you look my way, and then the world slowly turns to color. Your smile is like a ray of sun, bringin' life to everything. And to me? It's like you are my own personal sunbeam, sent down by the good Lord above to bless me. My life really started when I met you."

Sunbeam? A deep voice seemed to whisper in her ear, *"Are you paying attention, child? Like they say down there, here's your sign."*

I get it. Thank You, God. She couldn't help but snicker. "The answer's no, Cliff."

He bit his lip and nodded. "I see. Once again, J.R. won. Only this time, I lost everything I ever wanted. We'll head back to Lancaster in the morning." He proceeded to turn away.

"By the way, we need to get you some of those vitamin supplements to improve your memory. I hear the ones with beets are supposed to be the best for preserving memory and cognitive thinking."

He pivoted to face her. "Beg your pardon?"

"The answer was no."

"I heard that."

"But the question was, did I want us to break up."

His mouth fell open. "You don't?"

"Nope. I'm kind of looking forward to us sitting together, holding hands at the table today, and well maybe forever. But at the Christmas Day meal, let's get seats directly across from Maddie and J.R."

"Okay, but why?"

"So they can see that *we*," Lexi paused for effect, "we are the winners. Well, considering everything, I'm the one who took the grand prize, which is you. But you? Why, you caught God's sunbeam. J.R. didn't win, Cliff. We did."

"I, uh, I'm at a loss for words."

She reached for his hand and pulled him inside the room. "Then why don't you just come hold your Sunbeam?"

Lexi didn't have to ask twice.

Want to see where it all started?
If you liked *Sunbeam in Paradise*,
You'll love these...

Starlight in Paradise

Tracilyn is starting over in life with no plans to allow any man to complicate her future. But when an annoyingly attractive upstairs neighbor disturbs her solitude, will all that change? Scan this code to order *Starlight in Paradise, Christian Journeys in Paradise, Book Nine.*

Autumn in Paradise

Everything Annie worked for is gone. After losing both her job and boyfriend, she moves to Lancaster to start over. She soon finds herself in the company of two men. One is her mind's perfect choice, yet the other pulls at her heartstrings. Which should she follow – her mind or her heart? Scan this code to order *Autumn in Paradise, Christian Journeys in Paradise, Book Eight.*

West of Paradise

After three failed marriages, Teresa believes true love isn't on the menu. Until she meets red-bearded, ex-sea captain AJ Showers. It seems the man's mission is to make her life a wonderful dream. But when Teresa discovers the secret that AJ and the young neighbor woman share, will their romance sink... or will they sail off into the sunset happily ever after? Scan this code to order *West of Paradise,* a Paradise Sweetheart Romance Novella.

Treasure in Paradise

While researching characters for her upcoming book, Jasmine finds a real doozy in Josh Miller, a highly talented man who is doing his best to keep his skills hidden. Jasmine knows he's hiding something, so she keeps digging into Josh's life. Who knows? If she mines deep enough, she might find treasure. Click this link to order *Treasure in Paradise, Christian Journeys in Paradise, Book Seven.*

Road to Paradise

Beth may be young, but she knows what she wants – a once-in-a-lifetime fairy tale romance. After her first date with Anderson Warren, she believes she's met Prince Charming. But when his ex-fiancée storms into town like a tornado and leaves a swath of destruction between them, is there any way to put in back together? Scan this code to order *Road to Paradise,* a Paradise Sweetheart Romance Novella.

Want to read more of Chas's books?

*Get **Skating in Paradise** free*
when you subscribe to my newsletter.
Go to www.ChasWilliamson.com
to claim your free book!

Every day is a struggle for oncology nurse Tammy Kunkle. After cancer took both her little girl and husband, she's dedicated her life solely to helping others. But when Tammy visits a former child patient, she's introduced to a man filled with a warm, faithful spirit. Could it be Tammy has met her new future?

Download your free copy of
Skating in Paradise today at

www.chaswilliamson.com

Did you like
Sunbeam in Paradise?
Please consider leaving a review
for other readers.

For a complete list of Chas's books,
please visit the website at:

www.ChasWilliamson.com

Dedication

To Janet, my love, my life, my soulmate

Sunbeam in Paradise is a story of hope and destiny. As I wrote this, I couldn't help but think about all the ways God worked to bring us together, and how our paths were intertwined long before we met.

I love our story. From the first second I saw you, I fell in love with you, not even knowing your name. We married young and the deck was stacked against us, but we had love (and still do). Together, we've blazed a trail of love. Looking back, I'm amazed at all we've experienced and accomplished. And we did it all while holding tight to each other.

I could not write a story more amazing than ours, because our lives really are a *happily-ever-after*, true life adventure.

Thank you for picking me to be your husband, best friend and soulmate not only in this life, but for all eternity. I love you more than words could ever say.

This book, and my life, are dedicated to you, Janet.

True love lasts forever!

Acknowledgments

To God, for showering me with more blessings than I could ever count and for sending Your Son as a sacrifice so we could have eternal life with You.

To my partner on this journey of life. Mere words couldn't begin to describe not only my love, but the respect I hold in my heart for you. You truly are a treasure, like a *Sunbeam* God sent down, just for me.

To Demi, editor, publisher and friend, for always taking time, for coaching, challenging and helping me believe in myself.

To my grandchildren. You are the future and my prayer is you will always believe in yourselves and reach for your dreams. Remember, nothing is impossible.

To my fans. My wish is that God uses my words to touch and bless you. Thank you for being a fan!

To all who love the Lord. Let a smile adorn your face and may your heart overflow with kindness because, unknowingly, there are others who may see God's presence in you.

About the Author

Chas Williamson's lifelong dream was to write. He started writing his first book at age eight, but quit after two paragraphs. Yet some dreams never fade...

It's said one should write what one knows best. That left two choices—the world of environmental health and safety... or romance. Chas and his bride have built a fairytale life of love. At her encouragement, he began writing romance. The characters you'll meet in his books are very real to him, and he hopes they'll become just as real to you.

True Love Lasts Forever!
Follow Chas on www.bookbub.com

 Check out our website at
ChasWilliamson.com

 Check us out on Facebook at
Chas Williamson Books

 Follow us on Instagram at
Chas Williamson Instagram